A NORSE LULLABY

illustrated by Margot Tomes

A NORSE LULLABY

M. L. van Vorst

LOTHROP, LEE & SHEPARD BOOKS · NEW YORK

First Edition 1 2 3 4 5 6 7 8 9 10

Library of Congress Cataloging in Publication Data
van Vorst, M. L.   A Norse lullaby.
Summary: In this poem for bedtime, a mother and children await Father's return on a wintry night. 1. Children's poetry, American. 2. Sleep—Juvenile poetry. [1. Sleep—Poetry. 2. American poetry] I. Tomes, Margot, ill.   II. Title.
PS3543.A655N67   1988   811'.54   87-31058
ISBN 0-688-05812-4   ISBN 0-688-05813-2 (lib. bdg.)

*For Dorothy Briley
and for Dilys Evans*
M.T.

Over the crust of the hard white snow

The little feet of the reindeer go

(Hush, hush, the winds are low),

And the fine little bells are ringing!

Nothing can reach thee of woe or harm—

Safe is the shelter of mother's arm

(Hush, hush, the wind's a charm),

And mother's voice is singing.

Father is coming—he rides apace;

Fleet is the steed with the winds that race

(Hush, hush for a little space);

The snow to his mantle's clinging.

His flying steed with the wind's abreast—

Here by the fire are warmth and rest

(Hush, hush, in your little nest),

And mother's voice is singing.

Over the crust of the snow, hard by,

The little feet of the reindeer fly

(Hush, hush, the wind is high),

And the fine little bells are ringing!

Nothing can reach us of woe or harm—

Safe is the shelter of father's arm

(Hush, hush, the wind's a charm),

And mother's voice is singing.